scruffy bum,

fluffy bum.

Fast bum,

slow bum,

TAXI

TURTLE
TAXI

101
BUMS

Written by Sam Harper • Illustrated by Chris Jevons

Hodder
Children's
Books

Big bum,

little bum,

frizz bum,

whizz bum.

Mucky bum,

clucky bum,

laying eggs for tea.

Fuzzy bum,

buzzy bum,

what a busy bee!

Prickly bum,

tickly bum.

Ouch, that's very sharp!

Grumpy bum,

stumpy bum.

Watch out! Rumble...

PARP!

Bums in the jungle, bums in the town.

Bums in the
treetops,
hanging
upside down.

Bums in the farmyard,

bums in the park.

Lots of teeny-tiny bums,
glowing in the dark.

These bums love to **wiggle**.

And those bums like to **jiggle**.

This bum's feeling rather **smug**...

and this bum's **comfy** on the rug.

Some bums are rather **crazy**,

some are very **lazy**,

and this
one's very,
very, very
tall.

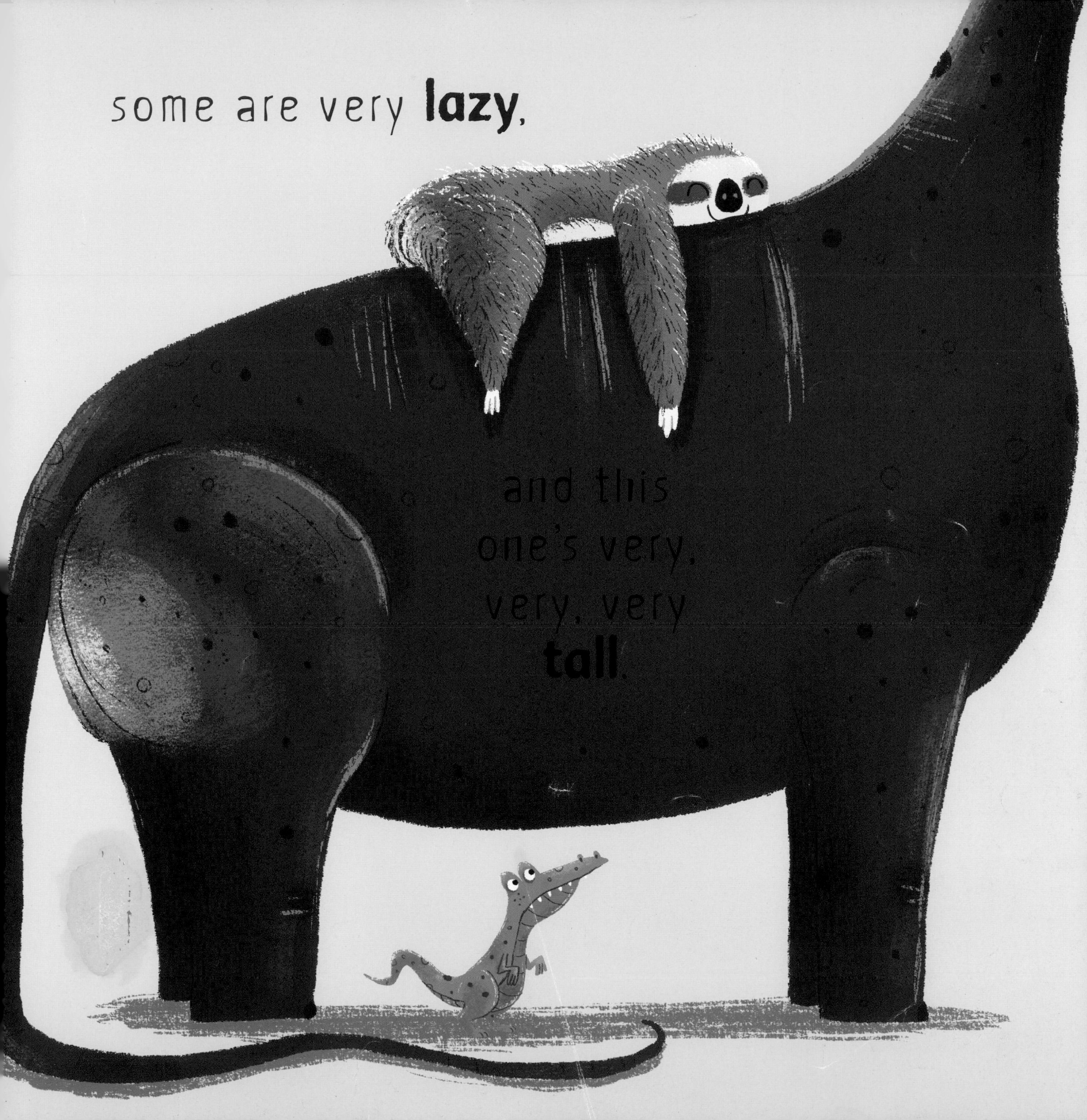

Chunky bums,

funky bums,
bopping in the sun.

Cute bum,

toot bum.

Poo-ie!
Quick – let's run!

Jazzy bums,

snazzy bums.

Get set . . .   ready . . .   pose!

Pink bum,

Spot bum, **dot** bum, **whiff** bum, **sniff** bum.

Dig bum, **big** bum, **stick** bum, **quick** bum...

Fluffy, scruffy, spotty, dotty,

chunky, funky, small . . .

It's time to shake your botty
at the jiggly wiggly ball!

There are **101** brilliant bums in this book! How many did you spot?

For my family
C.J.

HODDER CHILDREN'S BOOKS

First published in Great Britain in 2020
by Hodder and Stoughton

© Hachette Children's Group, 2020
Illustrations by Chris Jevons

A CIP catalogue record for this book is
available from the British Library.

ISBN: 978 1 44495 500 2

1 3 5 7 9 10 8 6 4 2

Printed and bound in China

MIX
Paper from
responsible sources
FSC® C104740
FSC
www.fsc.org

Hodder Children's Books
An imprint of Hachette Children's Group
Part of Hodder and Stoughton
Carmelite House, 50 Victoria Embankment, London, EC4Y 0DZ

An Hachette UK Company
www.hachette.co.uk
www.hachettechildrens.co.uk

One day Rex was stomping through the forest when he **scared a Troodon** called Travis.

RRROOOAAARRR!

"Aah! Don't DO that, Rex!" cried Travis.

"I can do what I want. I'm going to be the **biggest, scariest, noisiest** dinosaur ever!" roared Rex.

Next, Rex scared old Trudi Triceratops who was quietly eating leaves.

"I'll be just like my mum, and we're **not afraid** of anything!" said the young Tyrannosaurus rex.

Rex didn't have many friends.

He was just too big, too scary and too noisy to play with.

"Aah! cried Trudi. "Stop **doing** that Rex or you might be sorry."

"I'm **not afraid** of anything!" roared Rex. "I'm going to be the **biggest, scariest, noisiest** dinosaur ever!"

Everyone was **very tired** of Rex scaring them.

So, the next day Travis and the other Troodons came up with a plan.

Travis went to find Rex in the forest and said:

"You won't be the biggest dinosaur ever. My dad says there are **lots of dinosaurs** bigger than you!

Rex was furious! So he chased after Travis, roaring loudly.

Travis **raced through the trees** and led Rex down towards the lake.

"I can still be the scariest, noisiest dinosaur!" roared Rex. "I'm **not afraid** of anything!"

Rex skidded to a halt by a group of Troodons who were **gathered in a circle.**

"Look what we found," they said, showing Rex some **bright white things.**

"What ARE they?" whispered Rex.

The bright white things were flowers, but few dinosaurs had ever seen them before.

BBBUZZZZ!

Suddenly, a low humming sound came from inside the flower.

"Aaahhh!" bellowed Rex, backing away.

"Buzzzz, buzz!" said the flower again,
and Rex ran shrieking into the trees.

"Look!" said Travis. "It's just a little stripy thing," and a **buzzy bee** crawled out of the flower.

"Rex was so scared! We're **not afraid of him** now," laughed the Troodons.

BBBUZZZZ!

But Rex was too far away to hear them. He ran and ran and ran until he found Trudi Triceratops.

Rex told Trudi all about the **buzzing white** things.

So Trudi decided to go to the lake and **see for herself.**

Rex watched from behind a rock
as Trudi walked closer to the lake.

He could see the white flowers
and the stripy buzzing things.
"What are they?" Rex whispered.

"Aaah, these are flowers!" said the wise, old Triceratops. "You'll see many more of these as the world begins to change."

"And these buzzy things are bees. They help the flowers to grow. There's nothing scary here," said Trudi.

BBBUZZZZ!

Rex sat quietly on a rock looking around him.

"But I WAS scared," said Rex to himself. "And I'm not supposed to be afraid of anything!"

"Yeah!" shouted Travis popping up behind Rex. "Terrible T rex is scared of flowers. Ha, ha!"

"Everyone is **scared of something,**" said Trudi, moving closer. "But it isn't nice to be teased about it."

BBBWWWA

"But Rex **teased** us all the time," replied Travis. "And he was always scaring us with his roaring."

Suddenly, a **deafening noise** rocked the lake. It sounded just like a giant horn!

ARRR!

"Waaaaaaaaaah! What was that?" cried Travis, as he leapt into Rex's arms.

Seconds later, Piper the Parasaurolophus appeared out of the water and blew her head crest again.

BBBWWWWAAARRR!

"Ha, ha! It's only Piper," laughed Rex putting Travis down. "You were **really scared.**"

"So were you!" shouted Travis over the noise. "But everyone's scared of something!"

"So I'll never be the **biggest, scariest** or **noisiest** dinosaur," sighed Rex. "I'm scared of flowers, bees and loud noises!"

"But Rex, we **like you even more** because of that!" said the others, and everyone laughed.